WILLY AND HUGH

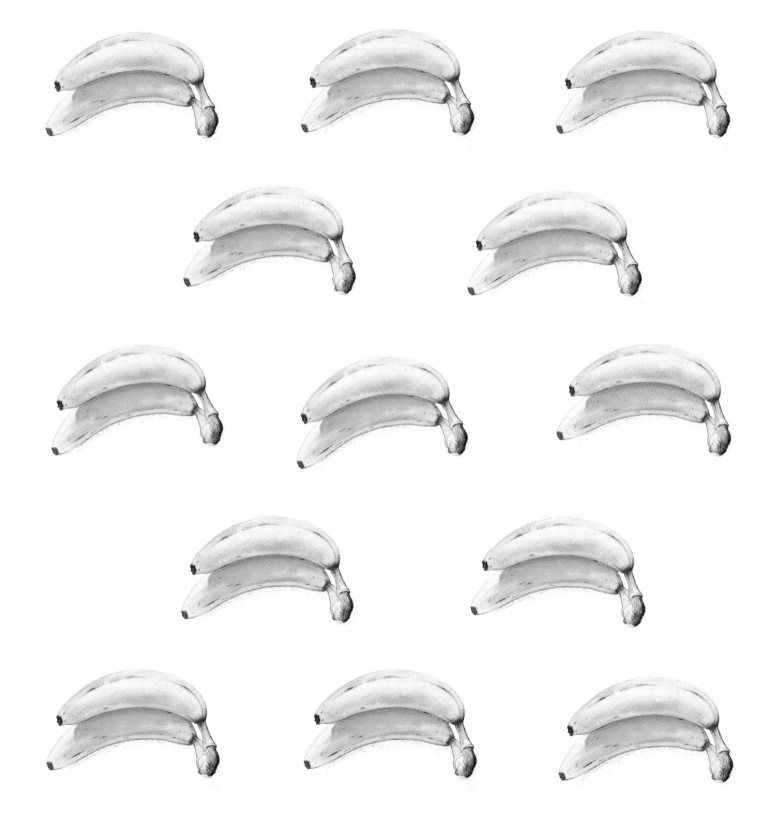

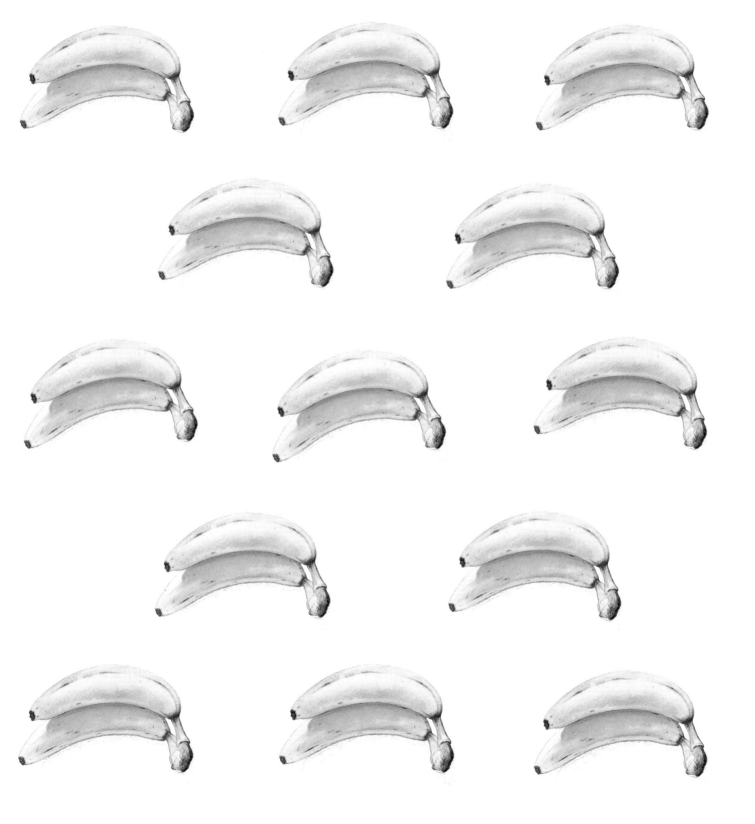

A Red Fox Book

Published by Random House Children's Books
20 Vauxhall Bridge Road, London SW1V 2SA

A division of Random House UK Ltd
London Melbourne Sydney Auckland
Johannesburg and agencies throughout the world

First published in Great Britain by
Julia MacRae 1991

5 7 9 10 8 6

Red Fox edition 1992

Printed in Singapore

RANDOM HOUSE UK Limited Reg. No. 954009

ISBN 0 09 997780 X

Anthony Browne

WILLY AND HUGH

RED FOX

Willy was lonely.

Everyone seemed to have friends.
Everyone except Willy.

No-one let him join in any games;
they all said he was useless.

One day Willy was
walking in the park ...

minding his own business ...

and Hugh Jape was running ... they met.

"Oh, I'm so sorry," said Hugh.

Willy was amazed. "But *I'm* sorry," he said, "I wasn't watching where I was going."

"No, it was *my* fault," said Hugh. "I wasn't looking where *I* was going. I'm sorry."

Hugh helped Willy to his feet.

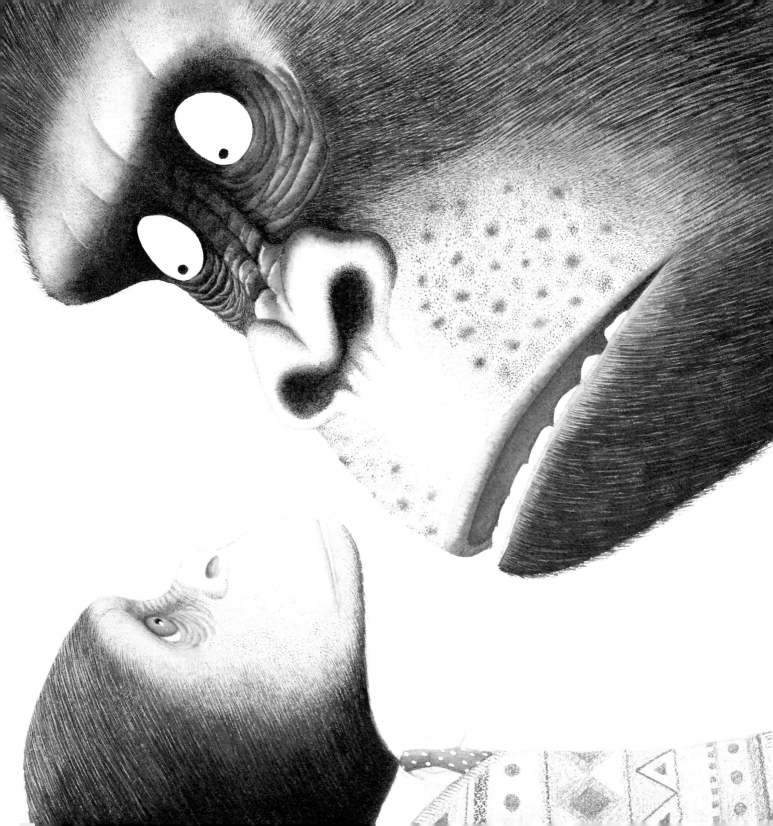

They sat down on a bench
and watched the joggers.
"Looks like they're *really*
enjoying themselves,"
said Hugh.
Willy laughed.

Buster Nose appeared. "I've been looking for you, little wimp," he sneered.

Hugh stood up. "Can *I* be of any help?" he asked.
Buster left. Very quickly.

So Willy and Hugh decided to go to the zoo.

Then they went
to the library, and
Willy read to Hugh.

As they were leaving the library,
Hugh stopped suddenly…

He'd seen a TERRIFYING CREATURE…

"Can *I* be of any help?" asked Willy, and he
carefully moved the spider out of the way.

Willy felt quite pleased with himself.

"Shall we meet up tomorrow?" asked Hugh.

"Yes, that would be great," said Willy.

And it was.

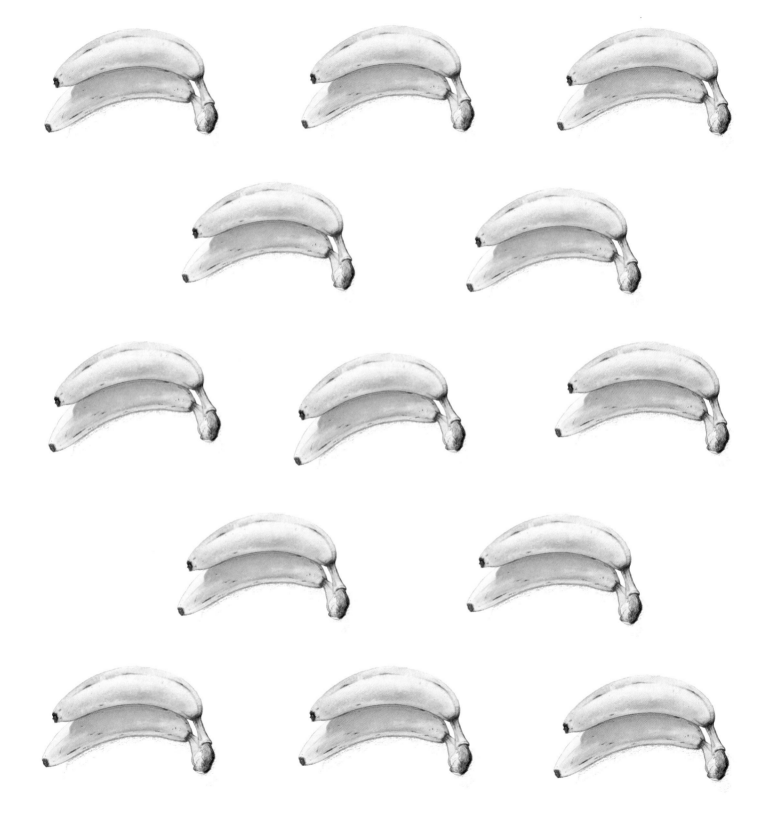

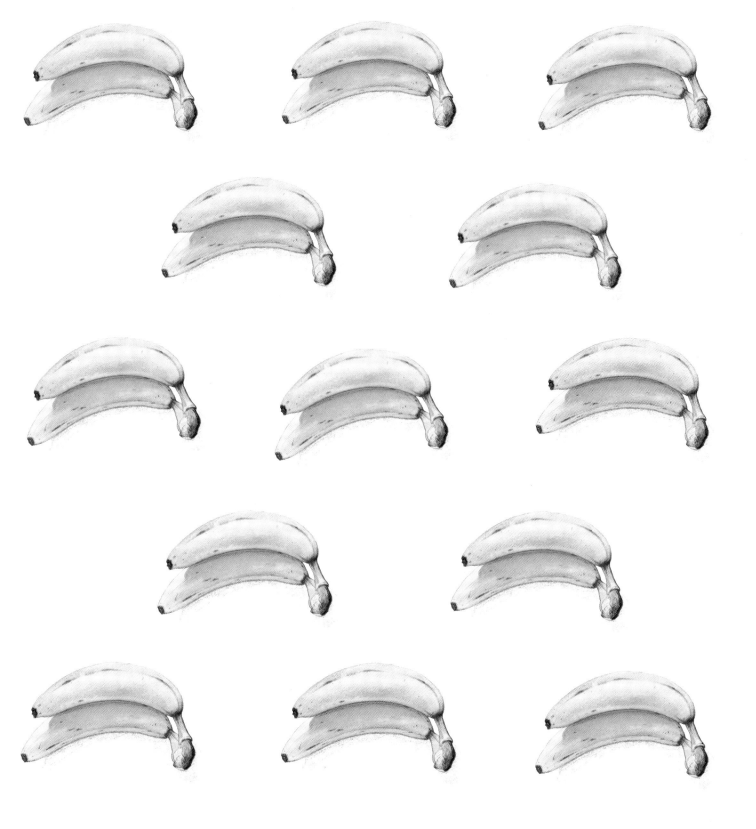

Some bestselling Red Fox picture books

THE BIG ALFIE AND ANNIE ROSE STORYBOOK
by Shirley Hughes
OLD BEAR
by Jane Hissey
OI! GET OFF OUR TRAIN
by John Burningham
DON'T DO THAT!
by Tony Ross
NOT NOW, BERNARD
by David McKee
ALL JOIN IN
by Quentin Blake
THE WHALES' SONG
by Gary Blythe and Dyan Sheldon
JESUS' CHRISTMAS PARTY
by Nicholas Allan
THE PATCHWORK CAT
by Nicola Bayley and William Mayne
MATILDA
by Hilaire Belloc and Posy Simmonds
WILLY AND HUGH
by Anthony Browne
THE WINTER HEDGEHOG
by Ann and Reg Cartwright
A DARK, DARK TALE
by Ruth Brown
HARRY, THE DIRTY DOG
by Gene Zion and Margaret Bloy Graham
DR XARGLE'S BOOK OF EARTHLETS
by Jeanne Willis and Tony Ross
WHERE'S THE BABY?
by Pat Hutchins